The
CHAMPION
CHARLIES

The
Knockout Cup

The CHAMPION CHARLIES

The Knockout Cup

ADRIAN BECK

Illustrations by **Adele K. Thomas**

RANDOM HOUSE AUSTRALIA

A Random House book
Published by Penguin Random House Australia Pty Ltd
Level 3, 100 Pacific Highway, North Sydney NSW 2060
penguin.com.au

Penguin
Random House
Australia

First published by Random House Australia in 2018

A catalogue record for this
book is available from the
National Library of Australia

ISBN: 978 0 14379 128 7

Cover image and internal illustrations by Adele K. Thomas
Cover design by Tasha Dixon
Internal design and typesetting by Midland Typesetters, Australia
Printed in Australia by Griffin Press, an accredited ISO AS/NZS 14001:2004
Environmental Management System printer

Penguin Random House Australia uses papers that are natural, renewable
and recyclable products and made from wood grown in sustainable forests.
The logging and manufacturing processes are expected to conform to the
environmental regulations of the country of origin.

To all the Matildas and Socceroos –
past, present and future.

CONTENTS

CHAPTER ONE

THE BLOCKOUT PUP

'Eight teams. Three days. One **WINNER!**' the announcer's voice boomed out around AAMI Park. 'It's time to reveal the competitors in this year's **KNOCKOUT CUP!**'

'Blockout pup?' asked CJ. 'What?'

Charlotte sighed. 'He said *Knockout Cup*.'

CJ and Charlotte were waiting in a gap between two full grandstands, midway down a slope that led into the depths of the stadium. They were standing with seven other kids their age. Each kid was wearing a different football uniform. And all of them were struggling to hear the announcer from their position.

It was half-time at the W-League. Matildas star Lisa De Vanna was DOMINATING in attack for Sydney FC, who were up 2–1 over Melbourne City. Fortunately for City, another Matildas star Kyah Simon had slotted a BRILLIANT forty-fourth minute goal! CJ was pretty sure this one was going to go down to the wire!

'Man, why can't we just get back to watching the game? Swifty hasn't even told us what we're doing here!' complained CJ. He was on his tiptoes, desperate to see what was happening out on the pitch.

'Perhaps Principal Swift is trying to make sure it's a surprise. But seriously, how exciting!' said Charlotte, jumping on the spot. 'How could we *not* have figured it out by now?'

'Figured *what* out?' asked CJ, as he took a running jump, then started scaling the side of the grandstand for a better view.

'Get down!' Charlotte swatted his ankles. 'And wipe that crazy look off your face!'

'Better view up here!' laughed CJ, as he leaped even higher, clinging to the side of the grandstand by his fingertips.

The kids from the other teams began noticing CJ's antics. A tall girl with super-short, bleached hair rolled her eyes and turned away, foot-juggling her ball. But it was the hulking guy with long curly red hair that really caught

CJ's eye. He wore an Akubra and Blunnies instead of football boots and was chewing gum with a mega snarl on his face.

CJ felt like he should say something. 'Hi. We're from the Jindaberg Jets. I'm just trying to see what's going on out there.'

No reply.

'Get down, before you hurt someone,' whispered Charlotte. 'Probably yourself.'

The kid with the hat grinned – revealing chunky metal braces – then spat his chewing gum.

DOOOING!

The little dollop struck CJ on the forehead. How **RUDE!**

'The moment has come!' continued the announcer out on the pitch. 'Representing

Finlay River FC, please welcome the Rock Lobsters' captain, Bruno Wells!'

A kid in a yellow strip ran out onto the pitch. He got a little cheer as he waved to the crowd.

'From Bindle Bay FC, please welcome the Bull Sharks' captain, Nicki Cruise!'

The blonde-haired girl effortlessly foot-juggled the ball as she ran onto the pitch. There was a bigger cheer. The crowd were impressed.

'Reckon people call her Tricky Nicki?' asked CJ.

'If they don't, they should,' replied Charlotte.

'And from Wombat Creek FC, last year's winners and therefore this year's hosts, please welcome the Wombats' captain, Damien Pratt!'

Damien adjusted his Akubra hat and strode out onto the pitch, but not before turning back to CJ and Charlotte, 'Most people call me Dirty Damo.'

I don't want to know why, thought CJ.

The sun caught Dirty Damo's braces and the reflection blinded CJ. As he shielded his face he lost his balance.

'Whoa!' CJ fell. He landed ON TOP of Charlotte, but she managed to steady herself using the grandstand. CJ clung onto Charlotte's head and ended up riding her shoulders like a horse.

'Dingbat! Get your butt out of my face.'

'And from Jindaberg FC . . .'

'CJ, seriously!' shrieked Charlotte, as she tried to SHAKE HIM OFF.

'Careful, I'm caught on something.' He couldn't help laughing as he wriggled around, trying to swing his leg free.

'. . . please welcome the Jets' co-captains, Charlotte Alessi and Charles "CJ" Jackson!'

'That's us!' exclaimed CJ.

'Well, get down and we'll get out there,' snapped Charlotte, trying to buck him off. CJ wasn't budging.

'My laces are caught on your ponytail!'

'Charlotte and CJ?' called the announcer once more.

They had to go.

Charlotte entered the pitch with CJ **ON HER SHOULDERS**. Laughs echoed around the stadium. CJ waved as if he was the Queen in the royal chariot and the crowd cheered loudly.

'This is so *not* how I pictured my AAMI Park debut,' complained Charlotte.

'I always know how to make an entrance!' laughed CJ, blowing kisses to the stands. 'Giddy up, Charlotte!'

Charlotte took CJ over to the line-up of players. He finally got his laces free and jumped down. As the remaining captains were announced, CJ took in the size of the stadium. It was MAGNIFICENT. Somehow it looked even better inside than it did from the outside, with all the football shapes lit up at night. But best of all, CJ suddenly noticed he was on the big screen. As he stared up at himself he went cross-eyed, which encouraged even more laughs from the crowd.

'I *hate* it when you have an audience,' groaned Charlotte.

The announcer stood in front of the kids, beside an object half his height, covered in a red cloth. 'All of these talented young footballers' teams – eight in total – have been selected to compete in next weekend's Knockout Cup!'

The announcer pulled away the red cloth and revealed a large golden trophy.

'Who will win it this year?'

'Give me a J!' shouted out a voice from the stands.

The crowd turned their heads, trying to locate where the voice was coming from. But CJ already knew: from his best mate, Benji. CJ and Charlotte had left Benji and Lexi in the front row of the northern end of the stadium.

'I said give me a J!' yelled Benji, again. This time he was standing in his seat.

'J!' replied the crowd, a little confused.

'Give me an E!' continued Benji, and he spun a full 360 on one foot. Lexi was capturing it all on the school iPad, but she needn't have bothered – the AAMI Park cameras had Benji on the big screen.

'E!' echoed the crowd.

CJ smiled. Even Charlotte cracked a grin.

'Now give me a T . . . S!' hollered Benji, with a little wiggle of his hips.

'T! S!'

'What does it spell?'

'JETS!'

'And who's going to win the Knockout Cup?'

'JETS!' replied the crowd once more.

'Yeeeeeah!' cheered Benji, before executing a perfect BACKFLIP! The crowd went wild.

Dirty Damo leaned out from the line-up, loomed over at CJ and Charlotte and said, 'Ain't he sweet? Gonna be extra fun beating you, city suckers!'

'What a charmer,' muttered Charlotte.

CJ wasn't too fussed about Dirty Damo. He had his eyes fixed on the shiny Knockout Cup. After next weekend . . . it would belong to the Jets!

CHAPTER TWO

WASSUP CUP?

'We can **WIN** the Knockout Cup, but the first step is **PERFECT PREP**,' said Charlotte, as she dumped a tall stack of papers in the middle of the Jets. The whole team were sitting cross-legged on the school pitch, eager to start Wednesday's training. 'So, over these last three days I've created some new set plays. **A HUNDRED** of them to be exact.'

The group muttered, unsure if she was serious, but CJ believed it. Charlotte had pen stains on her hands, reddened eyes and her super slick ponytail was a little frayed – for the first time **EVER**.

'No-one said there'd be *reading*,' grunted the Paulveriser, whose last book report was on Mr Tickle. And he'd failed.

'Nice one, Charlotte.' CJ jumped to his feet. 'But first, let's boot the ball around a bit!'

The other Jets agreed, getting up to join him. Lexi began filming the scene on the iPad. Garlic – the school groundsman Baldock's dog – ran onto the pitch and started sprinting in circles around the group.

'**SIT DOWN!**' yelled Charlotte. '**NOW!**'

Everyone FROZE. Which was unfortunate because Garlic had begun peeing on the grass and the sudden silence meant his piddling noise seemed EXTRA LOUD.

Charlotte glared at the group.

The piddling continued.

Everyone stared at Garlic. Including Charlotte.

More piddling.

The dog looked back at them sheepishly.

Charlotte was having a tough time maintaining her fierce expression with the distracting noise continuing in the background. Then Garlic finished up and bounded over to her. Charlotte's face softened. She took a breath and smoothed down her hair. 'Okay, everyone. I know this might seem over the top, but I really think this is an opportunity to prove ourselves. Big time. Don't you agree?'

'Yeah!' replied Fahad.

'Woohoo!' cried both May and Antonio.

'Let's kick some butt!' said Benji.

'Totally!' CJ mimed a massive kick and his boot came flying off. It hit the Captain Jindaberg statue in the forehead, then bounced onto the chicken coop.

SMACK! B'GUUUUURK!

In CJ's mind it was the perfect cross for a header, like Aaron Mooy at his finest. But judging by Charlotte's face, her mind didn't work quite the same way as CJ's. So CJ sat back down.

Charlotte checked her watch. 'I only have forty-three minutes before I need to get home and put out all the bins before dinner. So, *please*, let's focus on my latest set play. I call it NUCLEAR NAPPY RASH.'

'Ewww,' said Lexi. 'Sounds nasty.'

Charlotte's set plays were often inspired by her baby sister, Sofia, but this one sounded more full-on than usual.

'Yep. It *is* nasty,' confirmed Charlotte, gritting her teeth. 'Because we need to get ruthless if we want to win the Cup.'

CJ laughed. Partly because that was CJ's style and partly because Charlotte's killer stare was freaking everyone out. 'Well, personally, I'm more concerned about where we're gonna put the Cup once we've won!' said CJ.

The Jets started firing off suggestions. Benji – as always, inspired by the top five bestselling books list in his family newsagency – grabbed Charlotte's pen and a sheet of paper to scrawl down the team's best ideas.

TOP FIVE WAYS JINDABERG PRIMARY CAN SHOW OFF THE KNOCKOUT CUP. (AFTER THE JETS TOTALLY WIN.)

1. Use it as the SCHOOL BELL. Swifty could stand on top of the toilet blocks and bang on it till the whole school hears.

2. Train the school's chickens to lay their EGGS in it.

3. Use it as a HAT. (The Paulveriser's idea, so no-one disagreed.)

4. Run a hose through it and turn it into a fancy BUBBLER. Refreshing!

5. Parade the Cup around the school via DRONE, 24/7 for the WHOLE YEAR.

Hey, WASSUP CUP?

As the discussion continued, Charlotte fumed at the time-wasting. CJ took her aside. 'You wanna calm down? You'll do their heads in.'

'Calm down? This is huge! A whole weekend away, dedicated entirely to football!' said Charlotte. 'I'm tingling all over!'

'You're just noxious.'

'Think you mean *anxious*,' said Charlotte. 'And of course I am. We've got to step up our game. The Wombats have won the Cup the last three years in a row.'

CJ thought for a moment. 'Well, just like the warts on my feet . . . three's enough.'

Charlotte's face went a little green as she returned to the centre of the group and gestured for everyone to take a copy of her game plans. The Jets were slow to move. It got awkward. So instead, Charlotte grabbed the netted bag of footballs and dumped them onto the grass. 'Right. Fair enough. Maybe we should learn on our feet.' Charlotte started calling out directions and the Jets got straight up and began kicking the balls around.

CJ grinned from ear to ear, as he imagined himself kicking the Knockout Cup's **WINNING GOAL**. He was soon jolted back to reality when he heard a familiar voice from across the pitch.

'Fear not! I'm *finally* here, children!' announced their teacher and coach Mr Hyants, who everyone called Highpants, due to his (you guessed it) **HIGH PANTS**. The man was striding onto the pitch with his own stack of paperwork.

'Oh great,' complained CJ. 'More theory.'

'Be nice. He might have some good ideas,' said Charlotte. 'For once.'

But right at that moment, Highpants tripped and fell forwards. His paperwork **SPLASHED** into a large muddy puddle. He watched hopelessly as it sunk. 'No matter. I'm sure Miss Alessi has plenty of ideas too.'

'Oodles,' muttered CJ, pointing towards Charlotte's stack of papers. At that moment a gust of wind blew them all UP INTO THE AIR.

Charlotte ran about trying to save her work, ordering everyone else to do the same. It was like one of those TV game shows where the contestants have to grab money.

CJ noticed the school's chooks watching from their coop. Even they must have thought the Jets looked like a bunch of chickens with their heads cut off.

CJ sighed. What was it that Charlotte had said? The first step is PERFECT PREP. Uh-oh.

CHAPTER THREE

ALL ABOARD!

BEST. THURSDAY. EVER. The classroom was buzzing. Even despite Highpants gleefully springing a geography quiz on them.

'What's the capital of Spain?' Lexi asked herself aloud, mid-test. 'S, *obviously*.'

'Good one,' grunted the Paulveriser, scrawling down the answer.

'Quiet, please!' said Highpants, as he patrolled the aisles.

Charlotte had already finished her test. Never one to waste time, she put her test aside and started re-doing her list of new Jets' tactics for the Knockout Cup. She was pressing her pen so hard it was ripping the paper.

A row back, beside Benji, CJ stretched in his seat, trying to peek at Charlotte's answers. 'Psst, Charlotte, what's that weird-looking bug on your left foot?'

'What?' Charlotte reached over to check. This gave CJ a clearer view, but right at that moment Highpants arrived beside him.

'Eyes down, Mr Jackson,' said Highpants, as he inspected CJ's test. 'Dear, dear me. For the last three questions you've answered "Wombat Creek".'

'Just a hunch,' said CJ. 'But I'm pretty confident.'

Highpants let out an EXCEPTIONALLY long sigh. It must've involved his nose as well as his mouth, because all his long nostril hairs fluttered like a willow tree in the breeze.

'Something on your mind, Mr Jackson?'

'There isn't usually,' muttered Saanvi.

'Children, children, children,' said Highpants, in his cold, dry voice. 'Let me assure you, that if you've answered "Wombat Creek" to ANY of the quiz questions, you're *dead* wrong.'

SIGHS AND GROANS sounded around the classroom.

'Life's tough! Clearly, you all have Wombat Creek on your little brains,' said Highpants. 'I suppose I shouldn't blame you. This time next week, one of the eight competing teams will have won the famous Knockout Cup.'

'Give me a J!' cried Benji.

'If-anyone-gives-him-a-J-I'll-give-you-all-detention!' snapped Highpants.

The class stayed silent.

Charlotte put her hand up. Highpants nodded for her to speak. 'Can you tell us a little about Wombat Creek? Geographically speaking, of course.'

'Certainly, Miss Alessi. Wombat Creek is a five hour bus ride north,' said Highpants, referring to the state map on the wall. 'Near the snowfields. So pack your winter woollies.'

'Winning will warm us up!' said CJ.

'Let's hope so, Mr Jackson,' said Highpants. 'Now, back to geography. What's the capital of Poland?'

'P!' said Lexi. 'Or is there a silent Q?'

Highpants buried his head in his hands.

After lunch on Thursday, all the Jets lined up at the school gates with their camping gear. CJ had his mum's old backpack. Charlotte had a bag covered in her numerous Scouts badges. And Benji had a bag that FARTED with every step due to the amount of WHOOPEE CUSHIONS stuffed inside.

Highpants walked down the line, checking all the Jets were there. Lexi arrived late, struggling to carry her backpack. It was so full it looked like it was about to explode.

'Lexi, you sure you've packed everything?' asked CJ, cheekily.

'Just the essentials – three moisturisers, one hair straightener and a dozen packs of lip gloss.'

Charlotte grinned. 'Reckon Tim Cahill would've packed lighter when he moved all the way to Millwall!'

The school minibus reversed into position. It was decorated in green and gold crepe paper. As it stopped right beside CJ, the door opened with a PSHHHHH.

BALDOCK?

The school's grumpy gardener, Baldock, was in the driver's seat. His round frame just barely fit behind the steering wheel. He was wearing his usual gardening attire, dark pants and a grimy old cap. CJ didn't think he'd ever

seen him wearing anything else, and as always, Mr Personality didn't say a word.

'Don't stare, Mr Jackson. Baldock has a bus licence and will be driving us all the way to Wombat Creek,' said Highpants, before addressing the rest of the group. 'All aboard!'

CJ and Benji scored a row near the back of the bus. The Paulveriser took up most of the back row all by himself. Besides, he liked to play corners, and playing corners with someone the size of a BOULDER, is not particularly fun. So people tended to let the Paulveriser spread out.

Charlotte and Lexi sat in the row ahead. Before the bus even started moving, Charlotte was doing her homework. She explained that she intended to use all her free time at Wombat Creek to focus on football, so she had to get her studies out of the way. CJ could already tell that his own homework might *accidentally* get snowed on and lost forever. Such a shame.

Principal Swift appeared at the school gates and waved the Jets off as the bus started to pull out. 'See you in the Final! I know you'll make it.'

Garlic the dog howled into the air as they left him behind.

When the bus passed Benji's dad's newsagency, The Dancing Dads dance group were waiting. The group featured the fathers of many of the Jets and they did a little 'Go Jets' routine to send the team on their way.

Moments later, Benji kicked off the school song and everyone joined in at full volume. Lexi captured it all on the school iPad – it was a rollicking ride, even Charlotte was persuaded to put her homework away.

It took about an hour for everyone to settle down. In fact, the Paulveriser was so settled he started sleeping, with snores that would've passed for a BUSH PIG, all the while producing extreme amounts of DROOL.

Outside, the suburban houses became industrial buildings, which in turn became farms and countryside. The further they travelled the colder it got and – just because he could – CJ drew a BIG ROUND BUM on his fogged up window.

Then, five hours after they'd departed, the bus came to an abrupt stop.

THWACK!

The Paulveriser's drool splashed onto the back of CJ's neck. It was WARM AND GOOPY. CJ ducked down, trying to wipe himself clean by dragging his neck against the rail on his seat, but he only managed to stick his neck into some gum. 'EWWWW.'

'Oi!' said the Paulveriser. 'That's mine.'

The rest of the Jets stood to look out of the window, wondering why Baldock had stopped so suddenly. An actual wombat was shuffling across the road in front of them. The entire bus stared at the portly creature as it came to a halt beneath a large sign nestled among the trees. The sign read, 'WELCOME TO WOMBAT CREEK.'

'Children, I do believe we've arrived,' announced Highpants. 'Knockout Cup, here we come!'

FOOTBALL FUN FACTS - Tournaments, Comps and Leagues!

⚽ The FFA Cup is Australia's national knockout football competition and it's a ripper! It features Hyundai A-League teams plus clubs from lower tiers, including the National Premier Leagues. Adelaide United were the winners of the first ever FFA Cup. Go the Reds!

⚽ The largest football tournament ever was held in Bangkok, Thailand in 1999. It included 5098 teams and over 35,000 players. Wow! That's 70,000 boots!

⚽ The Isles of Scilly Football League is the smallest league in the world. Founded way back in the 1920s, there are just two competing teams: the Garrison Gunners and the Woolpack Wanderers. They play each other every Sunday, across a 17-game season.

Facts checked and doubled-checked by Charlotte Alessi.

CHAPTER FOUR

WELCOME TO WOMBAT CREEK

'Wombat Creek. Population 2005,' said Lexi, reading from the iPad as their minibus entered the main (and pretty much only) street. 'Known for its many wombats, its pumpkin harvest, its snow-capped hill and its terrible-tasting tap water. Ewww.'

'My guess: the wombats eat the pumpkins, pee in the snow, and when it melts it trickles down into the local water system!' laughed Benji.

Charlotte shook her head, 'That's one of the grossest things you've ever said, which is really saying something.'

Thick tree trunks lined either side of the main street, exploding into a canopy of leaves above. There was a post office, a school – consisting of just three buildings – an old sandstone pub, a corner store, the town hall and a bakery that promised the 'WORLD'S BEST SNOT BLOCKS'. CJ had no idea what snot blocks were, but he didn't doubt Wombat Creek made the best ones, because who else would want to make them?

'Right then,' said Highpants, referring to his phone. 'Our campsite should be at the end of the street, in the clearing beside the creek.'

Baldock grunted.

The bus passed an old poster on a wall that featured the kid who spat gum at CJ at the W-League game: Dirty Damo. He was posing with a very rotund redheaded man, who had to be Damo's father, and a curly haired blonde woman with a sickly sweet smile. All three wore Akubras. Along the bottom of the poster it said VOTE ONE PRATT.

'There he is, our friend with the hat,' said CJ, pointing Damo out to Charlotte. 'I'd love to wipe that metal smile off his face!'

'You and me both,' said Charlotte, scrunching up the homework in her hand. 'Whoops.'

'You okay? You seem a little . . . stressed.' asked CJ.

'Of course I am!' snapped Charlotte. 'Sorry, I'm just keen to get started, we've got so much to go through before our first match.'

The minibus pulled up beneath a tree at the *Wombat Creek Happy Campers Holiday Stay*.

Under Highpants' instructions everyone filed off the bus and waited with their gear. Baldock was in charge as Highpants strode into the little reception cabin.

Sprawling out in front of the Jets was a field already JAM—PACKED with tents. It was surrounded by bush on all sides except the left, where it sloped down towards a creek. The seven other Knockout Cup teams were clearly already in town, all set for the tournament. Various school flags and banners were on display, but the whole place was deserted.

WEIRD.

Highpants returned with a heavy-set woman who was wearing a nametag that said Marge. Her T-shirt read, 'CAMPING IS IN TENTS.'

'Right down there on the left.' Marge pointed. 'That's where you lot are!'

Highpants got on his tiptoes. 'Down there in the mud, next to the creek? One heavy downpour and we'll be washed away.'

'Campsite's full to the brim, lovey,' said Marge, shrugging. 'This is where old Pratty told me to put yas. He drew up a little map and all.'

'Pratty?'

'Yep. Percy Pratt. Wombat Creek FC coach,' said Marge. 'And also the mayor. Bit of a wheeler and dealer round these parts.'

'Right,' said Highpants. 'Well, I suppose there aren't many other options.'

'No, lovey,' said Marge. 'Not when you arrive so late.'

'Late?' said Highpants, his top lip getting sweaty.

'Yep. The other teams are already at the welcome dinner. Big slap-up do at the town hall.'

'Right. Well, thank you, madam,' said Highpants, checking his watch. 'We'd best get a wriggle on.'

SQUELCH, SQUELCH, SQUELCH.

The Jets stomped through their muddy section of the field. The roar of the creek was louder here and the cool spray hung in the air.

Winning will warm us up, thought CJ once again.

Everyone started putting up their tents. CJ had his old family tent. He yanked it from his backpack and it flew from his hands, bopping Highpants on the back of his bald head, then it fell into the mud.

'Sorry!' said CJ. 'Think the wind got hold of it.'

Charlotte grabbed the tent bag, shook off the mud, and handed it back to CJ. 'Get a move on, dingbat. It'll be dark soon.'

She'd been the first to get her tent up. Of course.

'Relax, this is one of those tents that sets itself up! You just undo the ties,' said CJ, fiddling away. 'Then wal-eey!'

The tent did nothing.

'You're the *Wally*,' said Charlotte, as she fiddled with the ties. 'I think you mean VOILA!'

CJ's tent sprung to life, like a self-inflating raft, but the tie was still wrapped around Charlotte's finger. She tried to flick her hand free. CJ attempted to help, but instead managed to push Charlotte INSIDE the tent. Unfortunately, the tent wasn't pegged down, the whole thing collapsed and started sliding on the mud. CJ dived for it, hoping to stop the tent before it slipped into the furious creek.

SPLASH!

CJ got covered in mud. He was no Mathew Ryan; the Socceroos' lightning-fast keeper would've stopped the runaway tent without so much as blinking.

'Auuuugh! Get me out of here!' yelled Charlotte, pushing against the tent material, desperate for an exit.

The bottom edge of the tent hit the water. Then it stopped.

BALDOCK.

His big hand was grabbing the tent from above, like a shopping bag. He lifted it up – with Charlotte inside – then plonked it back on level ground.

'Thanks, um, Mr Baldock,' said Charlotte, poking her head out the tent window.

Baldock gave the slightest nod, then with a solid stomp of his foot, he stuck the tent to the ground with a single tent peg. He limped off without saying a word.

When they were all set up, the Jets walked together along the Wombat Creek main street. Lexi complained about the ICY conditions as they headed to the town hall, a large building made of dark wood with high arched windows. Once inside, the Jets gazed around the big old hall, which was decorated in the eight teams' different colours. All the teams were sitting at their own long tables – the chatter was almost deafening. Everyone was tucking into platefuls of delicious food. It was like some kind of MEDIEVAL FEAST!

CJ's belly rumbled loudly, he bolted over to the Jets' table and stuck his hand in the mashed pumpkin. He took a massive scoop and slammed it in the vicinity of his mouth.

'Classic!' laughed Benji, sitting beside CJ who now had a mash goatee.

Mayor Percy Pratt – Dirty Damo's dad, who they'd seen on the poster from the bus – arrived to greet Highpants. He doffed his Akubra, revealing a shock of red hair.

'G'day!' He shook Highpants' hand, twisting his arm to be on top. 'PERCIVAL PRATT.'

The guy puffed out his red cheeks like a bullfrog, as though he thought just his name itself was impressive – and maybe it was in this town. 'Please sit, eat, and enjoy Wombat Creek's finest country hospitality!'

Highpants looked down his nose at Mayor Pratt. 'My email said dinner at 8 pm.'

'Oh no, always 7 pm. A typo, I assure you,' said Mayor Pratt, adjusting his colourful tie, which kicked up into the air over his bulging belly. He handed Highpants a glass of pumpkin juice. 'Cheers!'

As CJ was helping himself to a mountain of red jelly, Mayor Pratt leaned in between him and Charlotte. 'Make the most of the long weekend, kids. Just try not to take it to heart if you get knocked out in the first round.'

'Unlikely!' said Charlotte, her face screwed up.

'Yeah!' agreed CJ, who was now up on his feet. 'Your Wombats are about to meet their match!'

But the noisy chatter drowned out their words and the mayor was already striding over to someone a few tables away, with arms open for a hug.

Right at that moment, CJ locked eyes with another Akubra-wearing redhead: he was hunched over the table surrounded by his Wombat teammates. The mayor's son, Damien Pratt. Or, *Dirty Damo* to his friends. Although it seemed unlikely to CJ that Dirty Damo had many of them.

Dirty Damo chomped up a whole chicken drumstick. Then he spat out the bone in tiny little pieces.

PEW! PEW! PEW!

Even from three tables over CJ could hear the little pellets hit the plate. Dirty Damo grinned back at CJ and Charlotte with his MOUTH OF METAL.

Immediately, CJ tried to do the same trick with his own food, but CJ's dribble of jelly didn't seem quite as intimidating.

BLUB! BLUB! BLUB!

Lexi sat herself down opposite CJ, she was directly in his eye-line, blocking his view of Dirty Damo. She was filming selfie-style on the iPad. 'Such a cray-cray start to the Jets' Knockout Cup experience! How exactly does the comp work, guys?'

Lexi swung the iPad onto Charlotte.

'Um,' said Charlotte, seeming like she wasn't sure if this was a trick question. 'Well, if you lose, you get . . . *knocked out*.'

'Really?' said Lexi, amazed. 'Makes sense I guess. Later, viewers!' Lexi put the iPad down and started tucking into the pumpkin pies.

The iPad screen distracted CJ. It was pointing towards the corner of the hall.

Mayor Pratt was strolling towards the stage with a page of notes when he ran into Baldock who was returning to his seat. Pratt wore a smiley apologetic expression and moved on quickly, but Baldock stared at the man. The colour DRAINED from his craggy face, then he turned sharply and exited the hall, abandoning his dinner.

That was weird, thought CJ. Although the thought didn't stay in his head long, he was quickly distracted by more plates of steaming deliciousness that had been brought to the table.

Three courses later, most of them involving pumpkin, Charlotte suggested to Highpants that the Jets might benefit from an early night. She was determined to give them every chance at success. The Jets' coach agreed with her and he promptly marched them all back to camp.

⚽

After slipping and sliding their way through the mud to the campsite, the Jets were finally inside their tents and ready for bed. CJ was hoping to drift off to sleep to the sounds of nature: crickets and the creek, plus –

PAAAARRRRRP!

It was a NATURAL sound, but it was not NATURE.

PAAAAAAARRRRPPPPP!

All the kids in the Jets' camp burst out laughing.

'Whoever had too many beans, please show some self-control,' demanded Highpants.

Then a little nozzle poked into CJ's tent.

PAAAARRRRP!

The noise came from the nozzle.

More laughter around the campsite. Benji popped his head in and whispered. 'Whoopee cushion. Total classic, huh!'

'Love it!' laughed CJ.

PPPAAAARRRRP!

'Whoever that is, get to the toilet QUICK SMART!' yelled Highpants.

Benji sniggered. 'This is gonna be a fun night.' He ducked out of the tent and ran off.

As hilarious as farts were, and they were PURE COMEDY GOLD as far as CJ was concerned, he decided to listen to his iPod. He was desperate to sleep. His stomach was not only full of PUMPKIN SCONES, but also full of BUTTERFLIES. Their first match was tomorrow morning.

The Knockout Cup was about to begin!

CHAPTER FIVE

COCK-A-DOODLE-DON'T

I shouldn't have eaten that sixth pumpkin scone last night, thought CJ, as he jogged back to the centre of the pitch after another failed attempt on goal by the Jets. Their first game in the Knockout Cup was **NOT** going to plan.

They were down 1–0 to the Finlay River Rock Lobsters, and well into the second half. The Jets were in SERIOUS danger of being KNOCKED OUT in the first round. They had to turn things around. FAST.

The Jets and the Lobsters were playing on a pitch located at the Wombat Creek Dairy Farm. It was outside a rusty old milking shed with a creaky windmill. CJ was pretty sure that this particular section of grass was usually a cow paddock. The giveaway was the many cowpats laid out like LANDMINES on the pitch.

Highpants was not impressed. CJ had heard him muttering to himself as they'd arrived. 'Don't see Pratt's kids out battling bovines.'

Gum tree branches snaked out above. There were two stacks of hay bales, one for each team's bench. And the farmer was doing laps of the pitch in his spluttering old tractor with kids piled into the trailer among the pumpkins.

These were trying conditions, but they wouldn't stop the Jets *trying* to win.

A Lobster player, with chest hair spilling out of his jumper like a bouquet of flowers, had the ball in his defence. The hairy guy was dribbling, at SPEED, but the uneven surface made the ball unpredictable.

Standing on top of a hay bale, Highpants belted out some awful 80s pop song, 'Never gonna give you up!' This clearly annoyed Baldock and attracted some odd-sounding moos from the cows in the next field.

'Someone, take Hairy on!' cried CJ, struggling to make up ground.

Charlotte ran at Hairy as he crossed into the Jets' half. Mud sprayed up from her boots. She had a killer look in her eye, and for a moment the cows possibly sensed there was a bull on the field. But as she reached Hairy the ball hit a bump in the turf and went out of play, disappearing into a group of chickens.

The tall, skinny ref blew his whistle.

Charlotte kicked a clump of mud and grass into the air in frustration. CJ couldn't help but notice Charlotte hadn't been acting quite herself the whole game. Something was definitely up with her.

CJ ran over to Charlotte to discuss their game plan. The Lobsters were SUPER FIT and it wasn't easy keeping up with them. Fortunately, the delay in retrieving the ball was buying time for a breather.

'Maybe that big round mayor dude was right,' said Benji, running over to CJ. 'We might not even make it past the first round!'

'No chance,' said CJ, as a grin appeared on his face. 'Check out the windmill.'

'Um, why?'

'It just started spinning,' said CJ, as the rusty old blades rotated. 'Means the wind has picked up. And we're kicking *with* it.'

'So, stop gasbagging and get back in position,' snapped Charlotte.

The tall ref spotted the ball. 'It's over here! I'll grab it.'

The ref shooed away the chickens, but as he was jogging back onto the pitch a rooster ran at him. It jumped up, flapped its wings and struck its feet at the ref's BUTT! The ref bolted away, his long legs pumping. Now he had a hole in his shorts and his BRIGHT PURPLE UNDIES were revealed to all.

'Classic!' laughed Benji.

Once the ref got far enough away for the rooster to back off, Fahad threw the ball in. It hit Saanvi at her feet, she sprinted forward, then dished it off to May. Or at least she tried to.

but the ball sprung upwards on a divot in the grass. That's when a short Lobster player pounced – he intercepted the ball and dribbled it down the wing.

CJ noticed that Highpants had gone quiet. Usually, he'd take this opportunity to belt out a (not so) helpful song, but Highpants was bent over, clutching his stomach and making odd groaning sounds. He looked really pale. Was the stress getting to him?

CJ had to go after the short Lobster. He saw CJ coming and tried to pass, but CJ was just TOO QUICK. He nudged the ball away from Shorty then ran onto it, taking it back into the Lobsters' half.

'CJ! I'm here if you need me!' yelled Charlotte.

The two of them thundered down the field, zeroing in on the box.

COCK–A–DOODLE–DO!

The rooster was back, but CJ couldn't worry about that right now. He passed to Charlotte. She ran onto the ball, but it wasn't rolling true, hitting bumps in the ground.

The rooster crowed again.

Charlotte flicked the ball up into the air, smartly avoiding the pitch. Then she **BOOTED** it on the full just as the rooster crowed a third time.

COCK–A–DOODLE–GOAL!

The ball sailed straight through the fingers of the Lobster keeper!

1–1!

CJ ran to Charlotte for a bear hug, but over her shoulder he saw the ref running past, leaning back and holding onto his bottom.

Not far behind, the rooster crowed once more, then sauntered back to the chickens.

'Sorry. I didn't see the goal,' admitted the ref. 'Too busy being pecked on the patootie!'

'What?' cried CJ, stomping the ground. SQUEELCH! Straight into a cowpat. 'Eww'.

'But it was honestly a goal, *everyone* else saw it!' pleaded Charlotte.

But the Lobsters didn't exactly back her up. A couple even shrugged.

'We'll just have to play it again,' said the ref. 'Free kick to the Jets.'

'Come on!' exclaimed CJ. 'This is soooo unfair.'

The ref blew his whistle and rubbed his sore behind. 'I said, free kick! I suggest you be a good sport and accept the decision.'

The Jets had no choice. Charlotte – who looked **FURIOUS** – took the ball and slapped it on the grass just outside the box. The Lobsters made a wall of five between her and the goals.

All the other players bustled around, jostling for position.

Charlotte poked her tongue out a little. It was her maths-problem-face. It only lasted for the briefest millisecond, but in that moment CJ knew Charlotte's head was full of a billion calculations. She got Lexi's attention with a tap to the forehead. Charlotte was signalling that **THE HEADER CROSS WAS ON!**

Lexi screwed up her face, she didn't have a clue, but Benji whispered in her ear. She nodded. 'Oh right, you want me to do a header! Got it!'

Fortunately, there was no time for the Lobsters to react to Lexi revealing the plan, because Charlotte scooped the ball over the opposition's wall. Her calculations were perfect. The wind carried the ball through the air, straight to Lexi.

Off one, two, three steps, Lexi leaped high. The ball smacked into her forehead and she sent it **SOARING** above the two Lobster defenders lurking deep. It rocketed past the diving keeper and bounced off the base of the far goalpost.

BOIIIING!

'Nooooooooooo . . .' cried CJ, but he'd reacted too soon, because the ball rebounded **BACK** into the goals! '. . . oooooo waaaaaaay!' CJ corrected himself.

'Lexi, you star!' called Charlotte, running over to celebrate.

The ref blew his whistle! This one definitely counted. The game was **ALL TIED UP!** 1–1. For real.

Gearing up for a celebratory Jets stacks on CJ sprinted over to his teammates, but Charlotte stopped him. She pointed to the ground. 'Careful!'

'We don't want that kind of pat on the head,' laughed Benji.

'OM—JEEPERS!' said Lexi, holding her nose. 'It's the colour of their pumpkins!'

CJ expected some sort of song from Highpants to mark the occasion, but he was nowhere to be seen. Baldock was standing on his own, running his eyes over the goals, as though he was replaying Charlotte and Lexi's brilliant combo in his mind.

The Lobsters sped back to the centre for the kick-off. Their captain, Bruno Wells – who had thighs the size of TREE TRUNKS – was yelling out his instructions.

In an attempt to drown him out CJ shouted, 'One more, Jets. Just one more!'

Captain Bruno Thunder Thighs passed off to his teammate and drew Fahad out wide. The teammate passed back to Thunder Thighs and suddenly, the Lobsters had a clear run at goals.

Every Jet ran to help, but Bruno was TOO QUICK. It was all up to the Paulveriser now. He planted his big fat feet squarely on the goal line, and like a sumo ready to fight, he grunted at his ominous opponent.

Bruno stormed closer and took his shot. The ball skidded across the ground, dead on target. The Paulveriser didn't stand a chance, but he dived anyway. THUMP! He slammed into the ground so hard it must have registered on the Richter scale. Unfortunately for the Jets, his fingers were nowhere near the ball.

This was it. The Jets were about to be KNOCKED OUT in the first round.

But then . . . the ball stopped rolling!

'Huh?' said CJ.

It was stuck in a cowpat. The Paulveriser wriggled over and grabbed it. SAFE.

There was no time to marvel at what had just happened. With barely a minute left in the game it was still 1–1.

CJ called for the ball, just over halfway, running straight for the Lobsters' goal box. The Paulveriser thumped the ball and, with some wind assistance, it SOARED all the way to CJ.

There was just seconds left as CJ tapped the ball forward, drawing on the goals. But then a horrid noise sounded.

GRRRRRRRREEEEEEEER!

The tractor's engine grinded as its big wheels spun in mud. It was the type of loud angry noise that made your rib cage RATTLE. Everyone turned to look – everyone apart from CJ. He STAYED FOCUSED AND THUMPED THE BALL.

THWAAAACK!

The Lobsters and the Jets turned back to the action just in time to witness the ball sail straight into the bottom left corner of the goals!

GOOOOOOAL!

The ref blew his whistle. The full-time whistle! The Jets had won 2–1.

They were INTO THE NEXT ROUND!

High fives, bear hugs and crazy dancing all round! But no celebrations that involved getting too close to the grass. Eventually, the Jets wandered back to the sidelines. Baldock gave a single nod to CJ and Charlotte.

'Right, jolly good work, Jets,' Highpants'
voice echoed from inside a nearby portaloo.
'Now, children. I may be a few minutes in here.
All that pumpkin last night hasn't agreed with
my weak stomach.'

'Ewww,' said Lexi. 'TMI!'

COCK–A–DOODLE–DOO!

The ref ran past. He sprinted off into the
next field with the rooster chasing him.

FOOTBALL FUN FACTS – Unusual football pitches of the world

⚽ Estadio Hernando Siles in La Paz, Bolivia, is located 3637 metres above sea level. In fact, the high altitude made Lionel Messi vomit while playing there in 2013. Gross!

⚽ Igralište Batarija in Trogir, Croatia, is located between two World Heritage sites and both are 15th century fortresses. The Tower of St Marco is located behind one goal, while Kamerlengo Castle is behind the other.

⚽ The Float in Marina Bay, Singapore, is (as the name suggests) a floating platform in the middle of the bay! There is a grandstand on the bank that holds 30,000 spectators. Hope it never floats away mid-game!

Facts checked and doubled-checked by Charlotte Alessi.

CHAPTER SIX

CAMPFIRED UP!

As the afternoon sun began to fade, the Jets met around the campfire. The evening chill was setting in. Lexi had three designer coats on and Benji was wearing thermals – looking a little like a clown. The Paulveriser, on the other hand, merely sported a tank top. CJ had forgotten to pack any warm clothes, but found if he wore both his football tops he wasn't too cold. Just smelly. WHAT'S NEW?

The campsite owner, Marge, wandered by. Today her T-shirt featured two llamas. Via speech bubble, one asked, 'WANNA GO CAMPING?' The other llama responded, 'ALPACA TENT!'

Marge held her nose. 'Oi, city kids. Lay off the beans tonight, would ya?'

Benji and CJ laughed while Charlotte shook her head, unamused.

Walking past in the other direction were the Greenfield Geckos – one of the other eight teams in the Knockout Cup. They were very quiet and a few were limping. CJ had heard earlier that they'd lost to the Wombats.

'There's no point reporting them,' said a small kid at the front of the Geckos group. 'Their coach is the mayor, remember.'

Baldock grunted. He seemed grumpy. Well, EVEN GRUMPIER than usual.

'Reporting them for what?' wondered CJ aloud, as the Geckos moved on.

'You haven't heard?' replied Charlotte. 'The Wombats have a seriously dodgy rep. Bad sports, break rules and play rough. That kind of stuff. Is it any surprise given Dirty Damo is their captain?'

'Nope,' said CJ, watching another Gecko limp past. 'But we have a more ingredient challenge.'

'Do you mean *immediate*?'

'Probably,' said CJ, pointing across the field of tents to Tricky Nicki, who was foot juggling in front of a handful of her teammates. 'The Bindle Bay Bull Sharks.'

Tricky Nicki was like a CIRCUS JUGGLER. She flicked the ball from foot to foot then up to her head and round her back without even thinking. All the while she was mid-conversation with her friends. A MASTER at work.

'They beat the Western Point Pelicans 4–0,' said CJ.

'And we have them tomorrow,' said Saanvi. 'Yikes.'

In stunned silence, the group watched the Bull Sharks' SENSATIONAL skills with the football.

CJ stretched out his tired legs. Beside him Charlotte had her shoes off and was massaging her feet. On CJ's other side, Benji was rotating his shoulders. All the Jets seemed to be a little tender. Playing on the uneven farm pitch had taken its toll, yet they'd need to back it up tomorrow, regardless.

This would've been a great time for some inspirational advice from their coach. However, even if their coach wasn't spending unusual amounts of time on the TOILET, CJ doubted Highpants would've known what to say anyway. Their tetchy teacher didn't have a heck of a lot of football experience.

Across from CJ, Baldock stoked the fire. The flames danced in the grotty guy's dark eyes. Maybe Baldock would have to fill in for Highpants tomorrow. Would he know anything about football either?

'Don't look now but Dirty Damo's dad is doing the rounds,' said Charlotte, gesturing towards Mayor Pratt who was shaking hands with the Western Point Pelicans' coach nearby.

SPLOOOOSH!

Baldock stood up abruptly, threw a bucket of water on the campfire and growled, 'Bed!'

'Oh, okay,' said CJ. He glanced over at Charlotte who simply shrugged.

'Could use an early night anyway,' said Charlotte.

None of the Jets fancied an argument with Baldock, so they all got to their feet and began to make their way to the tents. Mayor Pratt arrived and started clapping. 'Well how about that, four teams knocked out and four teams remain!'

The Jets paused. Antonio laughed nervously.

'And here he is. Baldock – no doubt the Jets' mastermind! Apologies, I didn't recognise you last night.'

Recognise Baldock? wondered CJ. *From what?*

74

'How's life, old chap? Long time no see,' continued Mayor Pratt.

Baldock didn't reply.

'Kids, I hope you're taking care of my old friend!' said Mayor Pratt. 'If any of you have half his talent, the Jets might even give my Wombats a run for their money!'

Mayor Pratt laughed heartily at his own joke. CJ and the others didn't quite understand what the mayor was getting at.

'How's the leg? Dare I ask,' said the mayor, stepping back to inspect Baldock.

'Bed. Now!' grunted Baldock, ignoring Mayor Pratt, as he limped off. All the Jets hurried for their tents.

'Cheerio then!' said Mayor Pratt, still smiling, as he was left standing alone.

CJ's tent was FILTHY from the muddy incident the day before. Plus, he'd forgotten his PJs so he was sleeping in his football gear for the second night in a row. And he didn't have a pillow so he'd borrowed one of Benji's whoopee cushions. This was a genius idea, except that every time CJ turned his head he got a BLAST of flatulence in his ear.

But worst of all was the Paulveriser's SNORING. The Jets' goalie was in the next tent. The night before, CJ had fallen asleep listening to his iPod. Unfortunately, the battery was now dead as a dodo, so tonight CJ found himself trying to fall asleep to what sounded like a PIG with the FLU, who was wielding a CHAINSAW on a FREIGHT TRAIN.

Every time CJ turned his head he got a snore in one ear and a fart in the other. He hoped this wasn't a sign of things to come. There was every chance they'd be copping it from **ALL ANGLES** tomorrow too, against the Bull Sharks. Somehow, the Jets needed to find a way to beat Tricky Nicki's team if they wanted to make the Knockout Cup Grand Final.

CHAPTER SEVEN

A WHEEL AND A DEAL

CJ barely slept a wink. He got up at 5.30 am, upon hearing the rooster crow, expecting to be first up. He crawled out of his tent and was surprised to see Charlotte was already awake. She was sitting outside her tent knitting booties for baby Sofia, reading the current classroom novel and stoking the campfire with a stick she held between her toes. Just STANDARD LEVEL multitasking for her, but she looked FRAZZLED, CJ was almost certain she hadn't slept since leaving Jindaberg!

'Hey,' yawned CJ. 'What's all this?'

'Trying to keep busy,' said Charlotte. 'Feels super weird not being home to help out. I'm not myself. All night I've been trying to think up a more aggressive game plan for us, otherwise we'll be destroyed in our next match! I'm kind of freaking out to be honest with you.'

'Tell me about it.' CJ yawned again. 'Talking of game plans, we should relocate the Paulveriser's tent to the opposition's camp, maybe then we could all get a good night's sleep!'

'As long as we can exchange him for campfire wood,' said Charlotte, her breath creating puffs of smoke in the crisp air.

PAAAARRRP!

It sounded like a fart. CJ laughed.

Charlotte sighed. 'We know that's your whoopee cushion, Benji.'

Benji popped his head out of his tent. 'Classic!'

CJ noticed Dirty Damo and his friends wandering towards the Jets' camp. 'Um, hello?'

'Mornin' city suckers!' said Dirty Damo, his metallic teeth GLEAMING beneath his hat. 'Me cousin said to say g'day. Old teammate of yours. Remember Lenny Lincoln?'

Remember? thought CJ. *How could I forget?* The former Jets captain had caused them nothing but trouble since he left Jindaberg Primary at the start of the season.

'The family resemblance is uncanny,' said Charlotte, standing beside CJ and Benji.

'What's that s'posed to mean?' asked Dirty Damo. He and his mates were leaning against the big old tree that overhung the river. One of them was swinging a long stick, another was throwing a rock between his hands. Clearly, the Wombats were trying to get into the Jets' heads.

'You remind me of him, that's all,' said Charlotte, looking Dirty Damo up and down. 'It's not a compliment.'

'He doesn't talk youse up that much either. Ain't surprised,' sniggered Dirty Damo, as he noticed CJ's busted up, muddy tent among the rest of the Jets' lopsided campsite. 'Poor little city suckers. Just can't hack it out here, can ya?'

'Think you'll find we can handle ourselves when it counts,' said Charlotte, as she fronted up to him.

CJ could sense Charlotte was about to CRACK IT. Something about Wombat Creek had made her extremely FEISTY. Luckily, one of Benji's whoopee cushions emitted a loud PAAARRRRP, which distracted Charlotte's attention from Dirty Damo.

There was an old tyre tied to a rope, looped around the tree. Dirty Damo pulled the rope free and held the wheel out. 'We swing on this, right across the river in summer time. Youse brave enough to give it a go?'

'Ha! We're not that stupid,' snorted Charlotte. 'Not when the river's raging.'

Never one to turn down a challenge, CJ was already reaching for the tyre. But then Benji, taking everyone by surprise, used his aerobic skills to LEAP for it. His feet slotted into the wheel and he gripped the rope, ripping it out of Dirty Damo's hands.

'Woohooooooo!' cried Benji, as he swung like TARZAN off the bank and over the river. The bottom edge of the tyre skimmed the water.

'Whoa!' said Dirty Damo, impressed.

Charlotte stepped closer to the bank's edge, she seemed to be contemplating whether she needed to jump in the river to save Benji.

'Relax,' said CJ. 'He's totally fine.'

He was NOT totally fine.

Benji didn't have enough momentum. The tyre didn't swing all the way back to where it started. Instead, it swung AWAY again. Benji looked down, the blood drained from his face. He wasn't reaching either side of the river. As Benji fumbled the rope, he began SLIPPING.

Dirty Damo started LAUGHING. Then, so did his friends.

Benji FELL. He managed to land on one of the big rocks poking out of the river. Luckily his gymnastic-like mascot skills helped him to balance on the wobbly rock, but the water was fierce and the rock was unsteady.

'He won't last long,' exclaimed Charlotte, glancing around for some kind of solution.

CJ was about to dive in when Dirty Damo grabbed the big stick off his mate and put it in CJ's way, like a boom gate.

'Hey! We could use that stick to hook the rope and pull Benji back up here,' said Charlotte. 'Hand it over!'

'Or what, city suckers?' said Damo. 'You'll swipe your PT cards on me?'

'You don't wanna know what,' said CJ, who felt hot all over.

'And whatever he does, I'll triple it,' threatened Charlotte, stepping RIGHT UP to Dirty Damo, almost nose to nose.

Dirty Damo laughed again. He turned to the side and spat out his gum.

DONK!

It hit CJ on the forehead. CJ took half a step towards Damo, but the big guy started to speak. 'I'll let your little mate come back on *one* condition.'

'I'm listening,' said CJ, unable to take his eyes off Benji who appeared to be seriously considering trying to wade back through the current.

'Let's make a deal.' Damo smiled so all his menacing metal teeth were on display. 'CJ, if yas lose to us in the Knockout Cup then you quit football . . . for LIFE.'

'No way!' gasped CJ.

'This is ridiculous, just give me the stick,' said Charlotte. She reached for it but Damo held it further away.

'Uh-uh-uh!' said Damo. 'Not till you agree to me deal. And remember, good old cousin Lenny will be back in Jindaberg to make sure you live up to your word.'

'I'll be right!' cried Benji. 'I'm a master dog paddler.'

CJ wasn't convinced. The river looked like it was about to **SWEEP** him and his rock away.

'Come on. Seal the deal, eh?' said Damo. 'Let's shake on it.'

'Don't have much choice,' whispered CJ to Charlotte. 'Besides, we may not even end up playing them.'

'That's not the point,' said Charlotte.

CJ took a deep breath, then reached out to shake hands. Dirty Damo hocked up something **NASTY** and spat it into his palm. Eeew. The Wombat Creek kids cackled. Then Dirty Damo reached out too.

'What's going on here?' called Highpants.

Everyone **FROZE**.

Even though Highpants appeared a little green around the gills, he could still strike fear into the hearts of children like few other teachers on Earth. 'Quit this tomfoolery now! We must retrieve Mr Nguyen quick smart.'

'Of course! I just made a deal with CJ to help,' said Dirty Damo, all smiles. 'Let's do it.'

Using Charlotte's plan, they helped Benji back to the muddy bank. Dirty Damo and his mates disappeared quickly afterwards. Highpants was **FUMING**, but then he needed to run to the toilets again. As he took off, he made

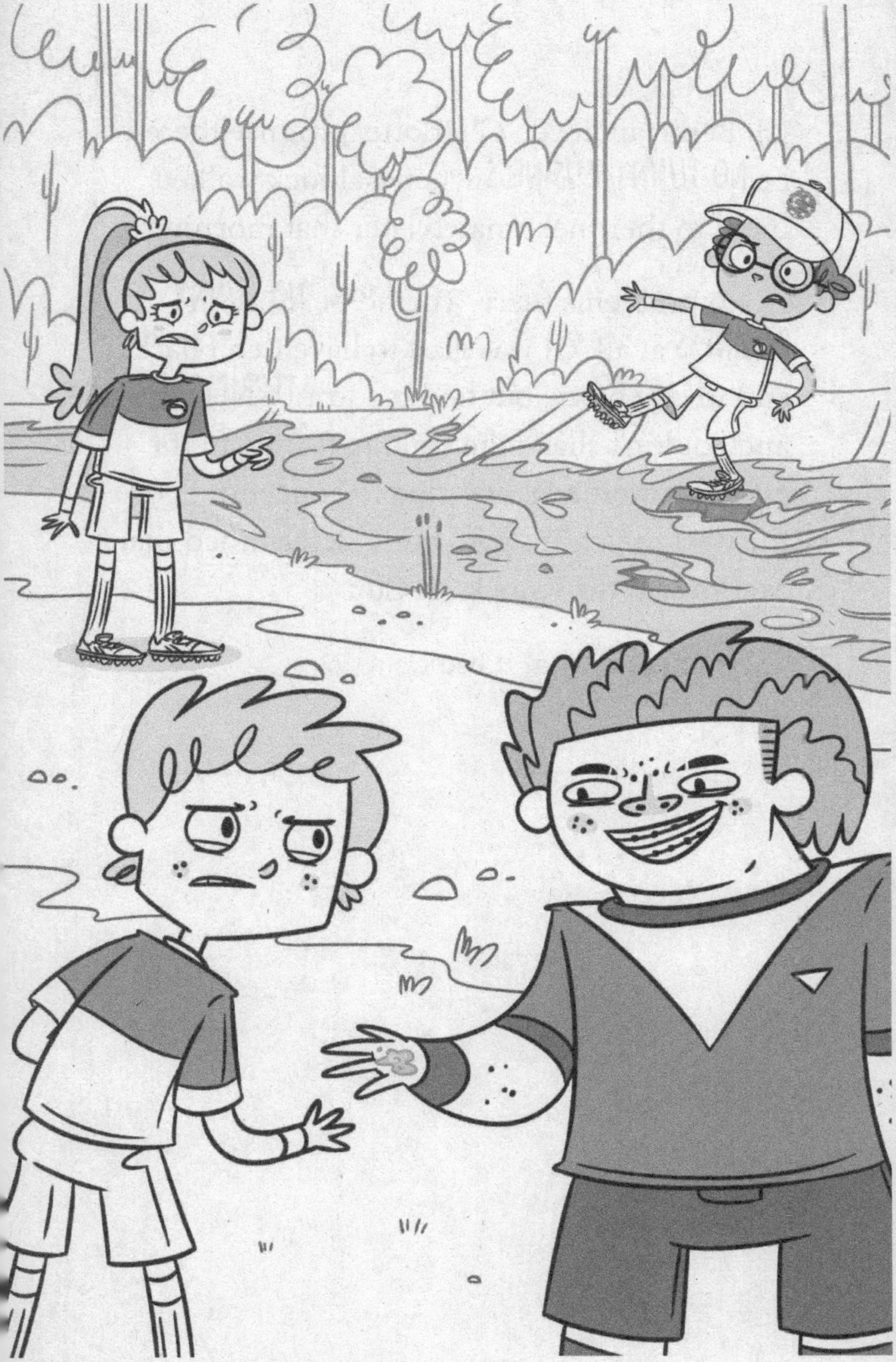

CJ, Benji, and even Charlotte, promise there'd be **NO FUNNY BUSINESS** when Baldock walked them to their next match later that morning.

No problems there. There'd be **NO FUNNY BUSINESS** at all. CJ was glad to have Benji back and in one piece, but he'd made a **TERRIBLE** deal and couldn't shake the sinking feeling in the pit of his stomach. He tried to concentrate on the next match instead, more determined than ever to win the Knockout Cup.

No matter what it took.

CHAPTER EIGHT

BEND IT LIKE BALDOCK

At 8.30 am, the Jets followed Baldock along the main street to Wombat Creek Primary School football pitch, where the big game was taking place. The mist in the air made everything seem SPOOKY.

The local school was tiny compared to Jindaberg Primary. It had three old sandstone buildings, trees everywhere and the only play area was the football pitch.

The Bull Sharks were already there when the Jets arrived. A Bull Shark football skidded towards the Jets. Baldock stepped out from the group and swiftly booted the ball back. He had impressive power, but the ball bent through the air and sailed straight over the top of the Bull Sharks.

'Not bad,' said CJ, surprised Baldock had any skills whatsoever.

THWUMP!

The ball slotted perfectly into the bag of balls the Bull Sharks had beside their goals.

'Whoa, not bad at all!'

Charlotte glanced from the bag, back to Baldock. 'Wow! Who *is* this guy?'

Baldock limped off towards the goalposts and dumped the Jets' equipment. He turned to the team and grunted. 'Warm-up!'

The Jets started jogging, their breath smoky in the cold air. It was freezing, the hair on CJ's legs stood on end, but maybe that was because they were running past Tricky Nicki and her team, who were doing their own, much more impressive, warm-up.

The Bull Sharks were slick. **SUPER SLICK.** There was a boy with a ponytail heading a football to himself – CJ counted 20 headers in a row so far. There was also a short girl who was foot juggling **TWO FOOTBALLS AT ONCE.** But it was the Bull Sharks' star captain, Tricky Nicki, who drew everyone's attention – and not just because of her striking short, blonde hairdo. She oozed determination and the way she was dishing out orders, you could tell she was a natural leader. She reminded CJ a little of Lisa De Vanna from the Matildas.

Tricky Nicki booted the ball up into the air and did a backflip. As she spun around she kicked the football. The moment she landed, the ball soared into the goals. SHEESH!

'Dude, how are we ever going to compete with these guys?' Benji asked CJ. 'Every one of them has MAD SKILLS.'

'You think? Reckon I could go one better than Tricky Nicki,' declared CJ, kicking his ball into the air, then running up to a bin to attempt a flip off the top. As with most of CJ's stunts, it didn't quite go the way he planned. He landed with one foot INSIDE the bin. And then the ball BOPPED him on the head.

Observing her co-captain's stupidity, Charlotte balled her fists in frustration. She gathered all the Jets in a tight circle for a pre-game pep talk, and she already had a fiery – some might say WILD – look in her eye.

'Okay, so we're one win away from making the Final, but we can't let that distract us.'

'Totally,' added CJ, as he removed a banana peel he'd found down his football sock; the leg that had ended up in the bin was making CJ even smellier than usual.

'Right now this is the only game that matters. The ONLY THING that matters,' said Charlotte, with a hint of crazy in her voice. 'At our best, I know we can beat these guys. Are you with me?'

The Jets nodded. After a roller-coaster season, they'd learned to focus.

'Bring it in,' said CJ. Everyone put their hands in.

'Whoooa Jets!'

As the team took to their positions, CJ pulled Charlotte aside. 'I didn't want to say this in front of the others, but to win this match we might need some kind of minor mirror ball.'

'Pretty sure you mean *miracle*,' said Charlotte. 'But yeah, you're right. One hundred per cent.'

Moments later a different, rather stern ref (one who didn't appear to be easily fazed by rogue roosters) blew her whistle to start the game.

Right from the kick-off the Jets gave it everything. They remembered their set plays and backed each other up, but they'd still been lucky to make it to half-time with the score 0–0.

Charlotte ran over to CJ as the Jets headed to the change rooms. 'I think we got our minor miracle, but there's nothing minor about him.'

She pointed at the Paulveriser. Charlotte was right (as usual). The Paulveriser was so fresh.

He'd been jumping about the goals like a BABY KANGAROO. In past games he plonked himself on the goal line and moved only when necessary. Today was a totally different story: so far he'd stopped THREE of Tricky Nicki's best shots.

'Amazing what a good night's sleep does for you,' muttered CJ.

Charlotte grinned. 'This is it, I can feel it. We need to keep it up. COME ON!'

She ran off into the visitors' change rooms, patting the other Jets on their backs.

CJ sighed. If this was how wound up Charlotte was today, she might actually EXPLODE if they were to make the Final tomorrow.

Baldock didn't say much during the half-time break. It could have been because Charlotte had so much to say that she barely drew breath, let alone allowed anyone else to speak.

As they ran back out to the pitch, Mayor Pratt stood on the sidelines clapping them onto the field.

'Looks like Baldock's got you all fired-up for the second half, Jets!' said Mayor Pratt, with a silly grin on his face. 'I remember some of his inspirational speeches from back in the day. A fellow like him would do very well in business!'

'What's he on about?' asked CJ.

'That old windbag? Who cares,' said Charlotte, her eyes locked on the ball in the centre of the pitch. 'All that matters now is the next half of the match.'

'Totally,' agreed CJ. He watched Charlotte as she gathered the team together for the second half. She really wasn't her usual sensible and super-organised self. CJ was getting a little concerned about her now. He was pretty sure she hadn't blinked in at least five minutes.

'Come on, Jets, positions *now*!' snapped Charlotte. 'I said NOW! DINGBATS!'

The Jets eyed each other in surprise as they took their places, they were used to Charlotte being bossy, but they weren't used to her being mean.

Tricky Nicki took the kick-off. She passed back to a longhaired boy who foot juggled three times before shooting off a pass that NUTMEGGED Saanvi, straight back to Tricky Nicki heading through the middle.

Tricky Nicki was so FOCUSED on goal it was as though nothing else existed.

CJ tried to catch her, but she was almost as fast as Socceroo speedster Mathew Leckie. She was at the top of the box in seconds, going for goal.

The Paulveriser was up on his toes – not a common thing – and Lexi was sprinting in from the side.

Tricky Nicki **BOOTED** the football. The Paulveriser dived. Amazingly, he got a fingertip to it, but the ball was still headed for goal. Then, in an almost slow-motion move, Lexi's foot **BLOCKED** it.

'Woohoo!' cried Charlotte.

Nicki kept storming in, but Lexi thumped the ball long and wide. Then she flicked her fringe and gave Nicki a killer smile.

This was CJ's chance. He raced for the ball alongside the longhaired Bull Shark.

I can be as tricky as Nicki, thought CJ. *I can win this for the Jets.*

He got to the ball half a second before his opponent and instead of passing out to May, CJ immediately kicked it up into the air, right **OVER** his opponent. CJ whipped past him and straight onto the ball, but another Bull Shark got in CJ's way. Ignoring Saanvi, CJ tried a second trick. But he tripped over the ball and fell **FLAT** on his face.

CJ was trying to do it all. And he'd ended up with a **MOUTHFUL** of grass. Then out of the corner of his eye he saw Baldock yelling from the boundary.

'Team!' called Baldock. 'Teeeeeam!'

TEAM.

He was right, of course. The Bull Sharks were an impressive bunch of show-offs, but they didn't play like a team. That's exactly how the Jets would **BEAT** them!

Charlotte must have heard Baldock too, because the moment she won the ball she yelled out a set play – at the top of her lungs – that involved every single Jets player.

'Listen up, Jets! It's time for TOYS-OUTTA-THE-COT!'
As usual, this play was inspired by Charlotte's
baby sister, Sofia.

The idea was simple. No-one hung onto the
ball, everyone passed it immediately – and it
worked! The ball zigzagged down the field at
SUPER SPEED.

CJ was last in the link of passes. He was
waiting at the edge of the goal box for Antonio
to send it his way. The Bull Sharks' goalie was
approaching, but with a simple nudge forward
CJ figured he'd create a clear shot on goal.

'Teeeeeam!' shouted Baldock from the
sidelines.

Oh yeah, team. CJ forced himself to ignore
the temptation to go it alone and passed to the
top of the square, catching the goalie out of
position.

THWAAAACK!

With her eyes popping and her teeth bared, Charlotte SLAMMED her foot into the ball and sent it HOWLING into the goals!

'Yeaaaaaah!' cried CJ, starting a Jets' STACKS ON!

Minutes later it was full-time. The Jets had WON 1–0! They were in the KNOCKOUT CUP GRAND FINAL!

The Jets jumped, hugged, high-fived, danced and CJ even did a few cartwheels.

'I'd wipe that smile off your face, CJ!' called Dirty Damo from the sidelines, who had just strolled onto the pitch to play in the second game of the day. 'We made a deal, remember, city sucker? If ya lose to *us*, ya have to quit football forever!'

'You've still got to beat the Termites to get into tomorrow's Final,' yelled CJ. 'Won't be easy.'

It *was* easy.

Dirty Damo's Wombats won 6–0.

It was JETS vs WOMBATS in the Knockout Cup Grand Final.

Not only were they massive underdogs, but CJ's football career was on the line.

FOOTBALL FUN FACTS - Underdogs

⚽ The West African country of Senegal shocked everyone at the 2002 World Cup in their first ever appearance. They made it all the way to the quarter-finals (!) before losing to Turkey 1-0.

⚽ Leicester City were the 2015-16 English Premier League champions, but at the start of the season they were given winning odds of 5000-1. Plus, the year before, they were nearly relegated out of the comp. What a comeback!

⚽ Some say Leicester City's amazing form was due to the skeleton of King Richard III being reburied in 2015 at Leicester Cathedral. Suddenly, the football team started winning. Spooky!

Facts checked and doubled-checked by Charlotte Alessi.

CHAPTER NINE

SNAGS, SNOW AND SOCCEROOS

Back at camp, the Jets were BUZZING.

They sang the school song 17 TIMES in a row, splashing mud as they jumped and danced around the campsite. By the end of it, even the Paulveriser finally seemed to know the words.

'Well, I'm flabbergasted! You did it!'

CJ would recognise that booming voice anywhere.

Highpants ducked out from between two tents. He was grinning. Something CJ would never get used to. 'My word! Even without ME, somehow you pulled it off.'

'Somehow,' muttered Charlotte, with a grin.

'Thanks, ah, Baldock for picking up the slack, as it were. I'll be back in action tomorrow, of course, to get the team across the line.' Highpants nodded at Baldock, then held his stomach. 'But I'm going to give tonight's sausage sizzle a miss. Don't want to tempt fate.'

A projector screen had been set up in the Happy Campers' car park. Kids from all the teams were carrying over camping chairs to bag the best spot to watch the evening's Socceroos match.

The Termites passed by the Jets' camp. The mood among their team was a little different. Getting beaten 6–0 will do that. A few of them were limping. One had scratches on his forehead. Another had the sleeve of her jumper ripped off. This was the Geckos all over again.

Clearly the Wombats lived up to their captain's nickname. They really did play DIRTY.

How do you beat a team like that?

Once all the Jets had found a viewing spot in the car park and the snags (and pumpkin burgers) had been served, CJ found himself in a little TROUBLE. He was standing on a trestle table near the barbie, holding a bottle of super-hot, make-your-eyes-water, you-gotta-be-crazy, call-the-ambulance, chilli sauce.

'Drink! Drink! Drink!' chanted the crowd of kids gathered around him. 'Drink!'

CJ could barely hear them and he was sweating BIG TIME. He'd tasted a few drips of the sauce and his nostrils had gone WIDER than the Paulveriser's Budgy Smugglers. His mouth felt like it was on FIRE.

'Check it out, everyone!' called Benji, slipping back into his old mascot ways. 'CJ reckons he can drink an entire bottle of chilli sauce. Classic stuff! He'll be breathing fire . . . from both ends!'

A little earlier, when Saanvi had warned him about the hot sauce, CJ had claimed he could drink the whole bottle. Unfortunately, the entire barbecue line had heard him.

'DRINK! DRINK! DRINK!'

As he lifted the chilli sauce to his mouth, CJ noticed Charlotte rolling her eyes at him from among the crowd. Further back he saw Highpants towering above everyone else, talking with another club's coach. CJ's tall tyrant of a teacher would soon spot him in action, but there was no backing out now.

CJ stomped his foot over and over, building himself up. He GRINNED wildly. After all, this was CJ's idea of fun, even if it was going to mean losing all sense in his tongue forever.

Closing his eyes, CJ squeezed the bottle.

But suddenly, the Socceroos commentary could be heard around the car park. The game was on! Everyone scrambled back to their spots to watch the kick-off.

Taking advantage of the distraction, CJ swiftly stepped aside and let the chilli sauce SPLAT onto the table.

Phew. Close one!

The night's big match was finally underway. CJ ran over to the other Jets and plonked himself between Benji and Charlotte. Benji was staring at the screen, zombie-like.

But Charlotte kept sighing to herself, restless. She couldn't seem to just sit there and relax.

Up on the screen, the commentators started getting excited. Benji and CJ were first to their feet as Aaron Mooy intercepted the ball in the midfield and started striding down the pitch. The whole car park jumped up as well.

'Come on, Aussies!'

'This is it!'

'Let's do it!'

Mooy spotted Tomi Juric in line with the left goalpost, a metre out of the box, but Juric had an opponent right on him. Mooy flicked it to Juric regardless. Juric got his foot to it and the ball bounced towards goal. Then STRAIGHT THROUGH!

Everyone in the stadium on screen CHEERED and everyone in the car park CHEERED too!

But then the stadium crowd fell silent. The kids in the car park listened in. It was called offside!

NO WAY!

The replay clearly showed Juric was equal with his opponent when the ball was passed, but on this occasion it was all up to the referees. The Socceroos were ROBBED! The commentators were outraged.

Sadly, the Aussie team didn't get another goal and they ended up losing 1–0. The match would go down as an honourable loss.

CJ walked alongside Charlotte as the Jets returned to their campsite.

'Bummer,' said CJ.

'Huh?' said Charlotte, a million miles away. 'Sorry, I can't stop thinking about tomorrow.'

'Totally. It's the big one!' said CJ, then he lowered his voice. 'Charlotte, now don't get mad or say it's another one of my stupid ideas, but to be in with any sort of chance, we might need to consider trying to beat the Wombats at their own game. Y'know, by playing a little . . . *dirty*.'

'I know,' admitted Charlotte. 'The same thing occurred to me.'

CJ was shocked. 'Really? You?'

Charlotte hung her head. 'Look, you know how much I want to win. And *you've* got even more on the line with that stupid bet you made.'

'Yep. It's true,' said CJ. 'But I was kinda hoping you'd tell me I was wrong!'

'Normally I'd be happy to,' said Charlotte. 'And *playing dirty* isn't us, is it? I mean, how would we feel if the Socceroos played that way?'

CJ laughed at the thought. 'As if! Don't be ridiculous!'

'Exactly. They lost tonight. Decisions went against them, but on every occasion they were good sports,' said Charlotte. 'They tried to win on their merits.'

As they arrived at their tents, CJ weighed it all up. 'They ended up losing in the end though, didn't they.'

'Yeah,' said Charlotte, sounding flat. 'Yeah, they did.'

'Well, there's nothing we can do now. Let's just try and get a good night's sleep. Catch you tomorrow,' said CJ, and he got into his tent.

The Paulveriser was snoring within seconds. CJ tried wearing his footy socks on his ears. This didn't make much difference, but at least it kept them warm. Maybe it wouldn't be too bad?

THREE AND HALF HOURS later, CJ finally fell asleep. One thought kept rattling round his brain, *tomorrow could be my last game of football EVER!*

The next morning as CJ poked his head out of his tent, he found that everything was WHITE. The other tents, the trees, the mud. Everything except the river was covered in a layer of snow.

'Get up, Jets!' cried CJ, as he ran around the campsite flinging snow about. The others quickly joined him. There were snowball fights, snow angels and even two snowmen – one tall and one round, that looked a lot like Highpants and Baldock.

CJ noticed Benji had written something in the layer of powder on the side of CJ's tent.

'One of your top fives?' asked CJ.

'Totally, dude. Meant to cheer you up if we lose,' said Benji. 'TOP FIVE THINGS CJ CAN DO INSTEAD OF EVER PLAYING FOOTBALL AGAIN.'

'And that's meant to cheer me up?' asked CJ.

'You'll love it!'

CJ read the side of the tent. He couldn't help giggling.

1. Professional STINK BOMB DESIGNER – make use of your many natural smells!

2. Forget The Dancing Dads, start a rival group called The Boogieing Boys.

3. Write a book on all your excuses for not doing homework. INSTANT BESTSELLER.

4. Become the Paulveriser's personal nose blower. Do us all a favour and save us from all the BOOGERS.

5. Start a 'Dollar-A-Dare' YouTube channel. Let's face it, you're going to do stupid stuff

anyway. Might as well make some cash out of it!'

CJ and Benji laughed, but then CJ noticed Charlotte not getting in on the snow action. She was sitting by the fire, tapping her feet up and down, checking her watch.

'Plenty of time till the big match, Charlotte,' said CJ, as he joined her. 'Enjoy the snow!'

'I can't,' snapped Charlotte. 'Too wound up.'

'But you're always wound up,' said CJ. It was meant to be a joke.

Charlotte shot him a look, then sighed. 'Not like this. It's weird, being away from home has meant I haven't had to help out with my brother and sisters, I haven't had to do any household chores, I haven't even thought about homework much. All I've had to focus on has been football.'

'That's a good thing, right?'

'It's doing my head in,' said Charlotte. 'I've played this game out a hundred times in my brain already. And a hundred times we've lost.'

CJ intended to draw a smiley face in the snow near Charlotte, but it ended up being yet another butt. She stared at him like he was a little loopy. As she often did.

'Come on,' said CJ. 'I'm feeling perspired!'

'Do you mean *inspired*?'

'Probably.'

CJ dragged Charlotte to the edge of the river. He started rolling up snowballs the size of footballs. And placed them on the edge of the riverbank.

Charlotte grinned.

Benji ran over. Then Lexi. Then the other Jets. Soon the whole team was lined up behind the snow footballs.

'What are we gonna do to the Wombats' butts today?' yelled CJ.

'We're gonna kick 'em!' cried Benji. 'Heeeeeeyah!'

All the Jets booted their snowballs. In a puff of powder the balls sailed into sky, leaving a trail of dust behind them, and each one splashed into the river.

Charlotte and the team burst out laughing.

'I sure hope we do,' muttered CJ. 'We'll soon find out.'

CHAPTER TEN

DOWN AND DIRTY

The Wombat Creek Primary School looked like something from a Christmas movie. The old buildings, tall trees and hill in the background were all covered in snow. The football pitch was the only thing that wasn't white because people had been walking across it all morning setting things up for the big game.

A large crowd had already gathered as the Jets arrived. The whole Wombat Creek community and the six other visiting teams were there to watch, all rugged up like they were on an Antarctic expedition. Wombat Creek decorations were everywhere. The Knockout Cup was a BIG DEAL for this little town.

As both teams lined up for the national anthem, Dirty Damo caught CJ's eye. Damo grinned. He looked like a ROBOTIC SHARK sent from the future to TERMINATE CJ's professional football career before it was able to begin. He pointed at CJ and then punched his own palm.

During the anthem, CJ's brain swirled. This was the biggest test his team had faced so far. Would the nerves get to them?

Mayor Pratt stepped up onto a little podium in the middle of the pitch and smiled. As usual, his tie flicked up at the end, over his enormous belly. 'Welcome, one and all, to this year's Knockout Cup Grand Final!'

The crowd cheered. There were also quite a few, 'Go Wombats!'

'This is sure to be another proud moment in Wombat Creek history! But what makes it even more special, is that to present the Cup today we have some VIP guests. Please welcome, none other than Steph Catley and Kyah Simon!'

The two superstar Matildas players stepped onto the pitch, both wearing their glistening gold tracksuits, each holding a handle of the Knockout Cup. They waved to the crowd. CJ was certain they waved at him!

'Dude, they just waved at ME!' said Benji, beside him.

Then the Matildas placed the Cup on a little stand beside the podium. For a moment the temperature didn't seem quite so cold – they were all in the presence of GREATNESS!

Mayor Pratt began interviewing both Aussie superstars, but the discussion soon turned into a speech about how wonderful Wombat Creek was, particularly the pumpkins. As he asked Steph and Kyah if they'd ever tried a snot block, CJ noticed Charlotte was wiggling on the spot.

'Still freaking out?' asked CJ.

'Uh-huh,' said Charlotte, nodding towards the Wombats. 'They look like a criminal line-up. This is going to be tough.'

'When the going gets tough, the tough get mowing.'

'You mean *going*,' said Charlotte.

CJ noticed she hadn't disagreed with him though. Was it really time to get TOUGH?

Mayor Pratt finished his speech and invited Principal Swift to say a few words.

'Swifty's here?' whispered CJ, glancing around to spot her.

The crowd parted for Principal Swift and she strode up to the microphone. Next to Mayor Pratt she looked like a stick figure. Plus, her long dark coat seemed very 'big city' compared to Mayor Pratt's Akubra and gumboots. She shook hands with the two Matildas legends then eyed off the crowd through her big round glasses.

'I'd like to wish both teams the very best of luck in the Grand Final. I'm sure you'll give it your all,' she said. 'But I just want to add one thing before we get underway.'

'I wish I'd brought my whoopee cushions,' whispered Benji. 'A quick blast would bring the house down right now.'

Principal Swift glanced at Benji. She couldn't possibly have heard him, could she?

'This Jindaberg Jets team is still very new, and in a few short months they've managed some *incredible* achievements.'

Charlotte smiled at CJ.

'But it's *how* they play that I'm truly proud of.'

At that moment CJ and Charlotte looked anywhere but at each other.

'I'm sure you'll see what I mean shortly. Happy Knockout Cup, everyone!'

The crowd clapped. Principal Swift gave CJ and Charlotte a little nod as she, the Matildas and Mayor Pratt left the pitch.

Highpants called everyone in for a last-minute huddle. 'It's not going to be easy today, but in the immortal words of Kanye . . .' Highpants adopted his best rap move, 'Now th-that don't kill me, can only make me stronger –'

CJ cut off Highpants by putting his fist in the centre of the group. Then Charlotte did the same. Then everyone.

'Whoooa Jets!' They all THREW THEIR FISTS to the sky.

This was it. DO OR DIE.

Dirty Damo took the kick-off. He thumped it back to a short kid with a buzz cut. The kid dribbled wide then sprinted between Antonio and May.

'Hold your defence!' yelled Charlotte, as Buzz Cut approached. She ran for him. There was a clash of legs and Buzz Cut GRABBED

Charlotte's jumper. Charlotte paused, expecting a whistle.

NOTHING.

'Hey! That was illegal!' yelled CJ.

The ref ignored him. Buzz Cut was getting away.

'All fair and square if you ask me!' said Dirty Damo, as he ran past CJ.

Then Buzz Cut BARRELLED into Fahad, knocking him flat. The crowd went OOOOOOH despite the fact they were basically *all* Wombat fans.

But still, no whistle.

'Oh, come ON!' argued Charlotte.

CJ was tagging Dirty Damo, who was laughing his way through the start of the match. Buzz Cut crossed the ball back towards them.

It was a little wide. CJ and Damo both went for a header . . . but neither connected.

THUMP!

OOOF!

They **SMACKED** into the ground as the Paulveriser, still as sprightly as ever, sprang into action and mopped up the ball.

Whilst lying flat, Dirty Damo kneed CJ in the back.

'Owww!'

Dirty Damo ran off.

Feeling a little ginger, CJ stood up. For a step or two he walked like a 99-year-old.

'It's becoming pretty obvious why they call him *Dirty* Damo,' said Charlotte, as she checked on CJ.

'The ref's letting everything go,' said CJ. 'We're in big trouble here.'

Then the ball was intercepted by a lanky Wombat. She cut through the centre and passed off to Dirty Damo.

Suddenly, the Wombats had **ANOTHER** chance to score!

CJ bolted towards the big fella. Damo was forced towards the sidelines, deep on the wing. It was just **CJ** vs **DIRTY DAMO**, but CJ slipped on an icy patch of grass. His legs slid forwards and he skidded on his bum.

Damo made his move. The only way CJ could stop him now was to stick his foot out and **TRIP** the guy.

A million thoughts zoomed through CJ's brain: how much the team wanted to win, how Principal Swift was proud of them, and – of course – how if they lost, CJ had to give up football . . . **FOREVER**. But last of all he thought of his mum.

And in that split second, CJ decided **NOT** to trip his opponent. He let Dirty Damo run at the goals.

Damo **THUMPED** the ball long and high. It went way over the Paulveriser's head and brushed the crossbar, but it went in.

GOAL TO THE WOMBATS!

The crowd erupted into cheers. 1–0. They could sense a Wombat victory already.

Around the field the Jets went limp. Some looked to the sky, others to the ground. CJ was in no hurry to get up.

'I could tell what you were thinking then,' said Charlotte, helping CJ onto his feet. 'You could have stopped him.'

'Could have. Did I make the right call?' asked CJ. 'It seems pretty clear to me that –'

'I know,' said Charlotte. 'That if we don't start playing dirty, we're gonna lose.'

CHAPTER ELEVEN

KNOCKED OUT

Steam was rising off the Jets at half-time, floating to the change room ceiling. Players were panting, gulping down water and treating their injuries. Some all at once. Everyone was feeling FLAT. And they were fast running out of bandaids.

'I have bruises on my bruises,' groaned Benji.

'I broke a nail!' complained Lexi to her iPad. 'These Wombats have crossed the line!'

Highpants burst in and stood on the bench. 'Quit your whingeing, children, we're still in this! At times like these I turn to the one and only Katy Perry.'

'Who?' wondered the Paulveriser. 'She a new student?'

Highpants used a water bottle as a mic. 'Baby, you're a fiiiiiiirework!'

'Been enough fireworks,' growled Baldock, slamming his tray of drinks down on the bench.

'Baldock?' said a flustered Highpants, eyebrows raised. 'Well, excuse me. It seems that our school groundskeeper has something to add. No, please. Do go ahead.'

'He's not only the groundskeeper,' said Charlotte. 'He used to play football. Mayor Pratt told us.'

'Long time ago,' muttered Baldock.

'Didn't get very far, clearly,' scoffed Highpants.

Baldock rolled up the leg of his pants. 'Cos I got m'self injured.'

There was a GRUESOME SCAR running down his calf.

'How?'

'Ask Mayor Pratt. Me opponent.'

Dirty tactics run in the family, thought CJ.

'Tough out there, today. Way I see it, you can play it their way an' maybe you'll be in with half a chance,' said Baldock, hands on his hips. 'But is that how youse wanna win?'

CJ tried to look anywhere but at Charlotte. He suspected she was probably doing the same.

'Your choice, stinky kids,' said Baldock, and he grinned, for the first time EVER!

'Indeed,' added Highpants, clearing his throat. 'What *he* said.'

Charlotte got to her feet. CJ noticed her uniform was a little torn and her hair was frazzled. 'Come on, Jets. There's just one half of football between us and the Knockout Cup,' said Charlotte, eyeballing everyone like some sort of evil hypnotist. 'We MUST start hitting the back of the net!'

'Totally! We'll knock the frost off it!' said CJ, backing her up. Then Dirty Damo's words

burst into his mind, *if you lose, you quit football, for life!* He shook his head at the idea. 'Besides, I don't plan on quitting football ANY time soon! Let's do this!'

The Jets jumped up and started making NOISE.

They burst out onto the pitch.

Outside, Principal Swift clapped loudly from the sidelines. She was joined by Steph and Kyah from the Matildas, but almost everyone else stayed silent.

Then the Wombats emerged and the crowd ERUPTED. There were scarves twirled, flags waved and streamers thrown. As far as the spectators were concerned, the local heroes had already won the Knockout Cup.

'We'll quieten them down soon enough,' said Charlotte to CJ.

'For sure,' agreed CJ. 'I get what Baldock was trying to say, but he's not out here copping it like we are. Reckon it's time to give the Wombats a taste of their own medicine?'

Charlotte had a TWISTED expression on her face as she scrutinised the opposition. CJ had never seen her quite like this before. She nodded. 'No choice if we wanna win.'

The ref blew his whistle. Charlotte took the kick-off and passed back to May. As she tried to dodge a spotty-faced Wombat, May dribbled out wide. The pimply guy took her out as he SLIDE TACKLED her. May fell to the ground with a THUD!

The crowd OOOHED. No whistle.

The Jets didn't even protest, by now they expected as much.

'Defend, Jets! DEFEND!' cried Charlotte.

The ref wasn't going to call anything. The Jets just had to weather the storm till the right opportunity presented itself. The Wombats broke through on a few occasions, but Lexi hassled them in defence. They weren't getting any easy shots away. Her BROKEN NAIL had really fired her up.

Late in the half, CJ was running on the spot: nervous energy OVERLOAD. He knew there couldn't be much time left. 'Get the ball moving, guys!'

Seconds later, Benji used his gymnastic-like mascot moves to send a through ball into the centre for CJ.

THIS was their chance.

CJ ran faster than ever before. His legs were a blur. He dribbled the ball straight through a gap between two Wombats and zeroed in on the goals. Defenders were on his tail, but he wasn't letting them catch him – even the ref was sprinting to keep up.

But then CJ skidded and OVERRAN the ball. He knew there were defenders right on him so he FLUNG it up with his heel. The ball flew over his head, bounced up at his chest, brushed his finger and then he flicked the ball back down to his feet.

He SLAMMED his foot into the ball, hoping to explode it into a GAZILLION pieces.

SMAAAACK!

The ball hurtled towards the top left corner of the goals. The Wombat keeper dived but she couldn't get anywhere near it.

GOOOOOOOAL!

Principal Swift cheered. So did some of the other losing teams in the crowd, but the WOMBAT supporters watched on in stony silence.

CJ's goal made it 1–1. The game would probably go down to a penalty shootout. With the Paulveriser in his career-best form they were in with a good chance of snatching **VICTORY!**

Charlotte and the Jets ran towards CJ – their eyes were full of excitement. He was a **HERO**. He'd kept their hopes of winning alive **AND** he'd **SAVED** his football career.

But it was based on a **LIE**.

'Handball,' said CJ, in a quiet little voice.

The ref had his whistle in, about to make the goal decision final. 'What?'

'It was handball,' said CJ, more clearly.

The whole crowd inhaled at once, every set of eyes darting from CJ to the ref. CJ's teammates slowed as they reached him.

'Dude? What?' asked Benji.

'CJ, what's going on?' asked Charlotte, panicked.

'I touched the ball. Out of instinct, really. I just flicked it down to my feet,' said CJ, dropping his head. 'But it was intentional.'

The crowd began to murmur. So did both teams. This was MOST UNUSUAL.

'You're sure, son?' asked the ref, almost admitting CJ could've got away with it.

CJ nodded, and showed where his hand brushed the ball.

'It's a free kick to the Wombats then,' said the ref.

The crowd cheered.

Dirty Damo ended up with the ball. He leered at CJ. 'You just kissed ya football career goodbye, city sucker.'

Damo hoofed the ball deep into the Jets' defence. He raced up the field for another attack, but the ref blew the full-time whistle.

1–0.

The Wombats had WON.

The crowd LOST IT. It was surprising the noise didn't blow the snow off the trees. Caps were being thrown in the air. People were hugging and high fiving.

On the pitch, the Wombats collided together. Dirty Damo was in the centre jumping about, celebrating. Then his teammates hoisted him into the air and he held two fists up to the SKY. 'Wombats are WINNERS!'

Antonio, Saanvi and Lexi had collapsed to their knees near CJ. They were red-faced and sweaty. No-one had an ounce of energy left, and it had all been for NOTHING.

Charlotte was glaring at Dirty Damo, who was jumping up and down.

What have I done? wondered CJ. He'd let down his entire team **AND** his football career was over.

FOOTBALL FUN FACTS - The Hand of God

⚽ One of the most famous goals in football history was scored by a superstar named Maradona (the player, not the old singer lady), and it became known as 'The Hand of God'.

⚽ The goal was scored in Argentina's World Cup quarter-final against England in Mexico in 1986. Diego Maradona punched the ball past the English keeper into the goals, and none of the officials spotted it!

⚽ Afterwards the striker claimed the goal had been scored 'a little with the head of Maradona and a little with the hand of God'.

Facts checked and doubled-checked by Charlotte Alessi.

CHAPTER TWELVE

SNOT BLOCK SHOCK

It wasn't much fun watching the Matildas' stars present the Knockout Cup to the Wombats, and the Jets left straight after the formalities. It was a quiet walk back to camp. CJ trailed behind: he was stinging from the loss, but also trying to get his head round the STUPID DEAL he'd made with Dirty Damo.

As they reached the camp car park, Charlotte slowed to chat with CJ. 'You okay?'

CJ shrugged.

'Been a full-on weekend, huh?' said Charlotte, with a half-hearted laugh.

'Yeah,' said CJ, coming to a stop. The handball incident was playing on his mind. 'Are you, um, *disappointed* with me?'

Charlotte stopped them walking. 'No way, dingbat.'

'But we LOST, Charlotte.'

'Yeah. But we can hold our heads up high, just like the Socceroos. The moment you admitted the handball I knew you were right. And I realised I would've done the same thing.'

'Seriously?'

'Clearly we were *tempted* to cross the line. And yes, me included. I went a little crazy being away from home and without my usual routine,' said Charlotte, shrinking within herself as she re-did her ponytail. 'I shouldn't have allowed myself to get wound up by those awful Wombats, but in the end we refused to play dirty. That's what's *most* important.'

'Especially given it was my last ever match,' said CJ. 'Cos we know Lenny will make sure I live up to my end of the Dirty Damo deal.'

Charlotte didn't have much to say about that, even she couldn't think of a way to fix the mess CJ had got himself into. So they kept walking.

In the Happy Campers car park, Principal Swift was standing near the minibus. Beside her was Marge the campsite owner, who was holding two large plates of baked goods.

The rest of the team were milling about enjoying the snacks.

'Here you go, lovies,' said Marge, offering the treats to CJ and Charlotte as they approached. Her T-shirt read: THE OUTDOORS IS UNBE–LEAF–ABLE! 'Try the pumpkin scones. Melt in your mouth, they do!'

'I've had enough pumpkin for a lifetime,' muttered Highpants.

'What are those?' wondered Benji, pointing to some pastries that OOZED yellow custardy stuff from the sides.

'Them? Why, they're good old-fashioned SNOT BLOCKS!' said Marge. 'Get 'em into ya!'

'Ewww,' said Lexi. 'They look even grosser than they sound.'

'They're a local delicacy!' added Principal Swift, licking her lips.

CJ grabbed one.

Charlotte rolled her eyes and smiled. 'How did I know you'd be first to try one!'

CJ took a big bite. It was gooey *and* crunchy all at once. WEIRD.

'He's gonna spew. Classic!' laughed Benji.

'Uh-uh. They're delish!' said CJ, giving two thumbs up with custard on his nose. 'I'm shocked!'

The rest of the snot blocks were snapped up quickly. Lexi remained unconvinced as she filmed the scene.

Soon after, the Jets packed up their tents and handed them to Baldock who was loading the minibus. Mayor Pratt and Dirty Damo were wandering the campsite to see all the teams off. At least officially that was what they were doing, but it was no accident that Damo was holding the Knockout Cup trophy.

The Pratts came over to the minibus. CJ turned away from them, pretending he was fascinated by the vehicle's tyre.

'You know what, it's been great to see you, old chap,' said Mayor Pratt to Baldock. 'For the record, I want to apologise for what happened all those years ago. I mean it.'

Baldock grunted, as if to say 'don't bother me' as he kept loading gear.

Highpants strode over, wondering what was up. 'Everything in order here?'

Mayor Pratt reached out for a handshake. 'I'm serious, Baldock. I really am sorry. Shake my hand. I want this to count.'

Baldock paused. He searched Mayor Pratt's face. Then shook his hand.

CJ made a mental note to get someone far smarter than himself to do some digging on

Baldock's MYSTERIOUS football past once they got back home. (Probably Charlotte.)

'Well, safe travels, all,' said Mayor Pratt, turning to leave.

Dirty Damo lingered behind and leaned into CJ. 'Don't forget the deal we made yesterday morning. You're giving up football *forever*, remember!'

Mayor Pratt paused, looking his son in the eyes. 'What was that, Damien?'

'Nothin' Dad.'

'What's this nonsense?' asked Highpants. 'Are you two talking about the regrettable moment by the river I witnessed yesterday?'

'Yeah,' said Damo. 'So what if we are.'

CJ sighed. 'A deal's a deal. I guess I . . . quit football.'

'That wasn't a deal. That was *blackmail*,' said Highpants. 'Besides, I caught you before you both shook on it!'

'You should know by now, Damien,' said Mayor Pratt. 'In business if you don't shake on a deal, it doesn't count.'

'But Daaaad!' complained Dirty Damo, like he was five.

'Don't *but Dad* me!'

CJ giggled to himself: *butt-Dad!*

'It's official then. Whatever silly deal you two made doesn't count,' said Mayor Pratt. 'And I won't hear another word about it, son.'

Dirty Damo stormed off.

Suddenly, CJ felt like he was floating. PHEW! And MEGA PHEW! He did a little dance on the spot. His football career WASN'T OVER! Woohoo!

Mayor Pratt laughed. 'After all, we want to see *every one* of you Jets back here next year so we can beat you all over again!'

'We'll see!' said CJ.

Half an hour later the Jets were on the road, aboard the minibus as it chugged down Wombat Creek's main street. As they passed by the bakery CJ was sure he spotted Kyah Simon and Steph Catley trying snot blocks in the window. Steph had custard dripping from her chin!

'Thanks For Visiting Wombat Creek!' read the sign as the bus motored out of town. Benji was already putting his whoopee cushions to good use. Charlotte was back to reading and knitting a baby beanie (seeming more and more like herself the closer she got to home), and Lexi was recording a clip on her iPad.

Just out of town, CJ spotted another poster of the Pratt family on the side of a barn. He vowed to be back one day to challenge the Wombats for the title. The Jets hadn't won the Knockout Cup, but maybe Charlotte was right and they'd proven themselves in another way. CJ couldn't help thinking it was just a pity you didn't get a **BIG GOLD TROPHY** for that too.

Highpants stood in the aisle with paper cups and a large thermos. 'Listen up, children! Marge made us all soup for the journey back.'

Highpants sniffed the contents. 'Oh bother, it's, um, **PUMPKIN**.'

'Nooooooo!'

READ ALL THE BOOKS IN
THE CHAMPION CHARLIES SERIES

Read on for an extract from
The Champion Charlies: The Grand Finale

CHAPTER ONE

EXTERMINATE!

It was either JELLY or ANCHOVIES.

Or both.

And Charles 'CJ' Jackson's toes were
SQUIRMING in it. The moment he'd kicked off

his sneakers and pulled on his boots – just before the match began – he'd felt the gooey, cold liquid SQUISH through his socks, then up between his toes. Pushed for time, CJ thought he'd be able to ignore it. But late in the second half of the game he still found himself curling up his toes to avoid the STINKY OOZE.

Someone was messing with him. And that someone was in the crowd: Lenny Lincoln. The gorilla with a mohawk. The former Jets captain. The BANE of CJ's existence (apart from maths, of course). Lenny must have snuck the icky mixture inside CJ's boots that morning. CJ often left his football gear strewn about his front yard, so the boots would've been easy to get to. Maybe CJ should've been thankful Lenny hadn't simply stolen them again.

But CJ had to ignore Lenny and his Hammerhead FC mates. NOTHING ELSE MATTERED right now, other than beating the Zenlake Zebras.

'Stick to the game plan, Jets! If we win today we're in the Grand Final!' cried Charlotte, covered in mud and puffing hard in the centre of the pitch. 'But lose . . . and our season's over!'

'Totally, Charlotte!' yelled CJ, running over to his co-captain, covered in even more mud, looking like some sort of swamp monster. 'It's called an *Extermination* Final for a reason, everyone. We need to EXTERMINATE!'

'Eliminate,' said Charlotte.

'Huh?'

'It's an *Elimination* Final, dingbat,' said Charlotte. 'Leave the details to me, you focus on scoring!'

That was music to CJ's ears. He didn't need to be asked twice.

The Jindaberg Primary School football pitch was packed with fans. There were plenty of people in Jets green and gold, but almost as many in Zebras black and white. Some kids were sitting on the chicken coop for a better view. One was even straddling the old Captain Jindaberg statue's shoulders. The cheering had been as DEAFENING as a crowd at a blockbuster Socceroos match. Even Coach Highpants' booming voice was struggling to cut through the roar. (Just for the record, Highpants was technically named Mr Hyants, but all his students called him Highpants because he wore his pants so high they defied the laws of gravity). The Jets coach was alongside Principal Swift and the school groundsman, Baldock. Both were blocking their ears as Highpants belted out, 'It's the fiiiiinal count*down*! D'ddle do doo, D'ddle d'do doo!'

This wasn't much help, but Highpants was right. Time WAS running out. There couldn't have been more than a minute on the clock.

The Jets had learned a whole bunch of lessons over the course of their first season together. They were clicking as a team at just the right time. Everyone was playing their role. From CJ's best mate, Benji, putting his gymnastic skills to good use by setting up unbelievable scoring opportunities in attack, to Lexi in defence who streamed back to block the opposition just as often as she streamed her viral videos live to YouTube. Even the Paulveriser (real name, Paul) had stepped up his game guarding the goals almost as fiercely as he guarded his party pies at lunch.

But despite it all, the score was locked at 0–0.